Sally and the elephant

Rigby®
A Harcourt Achieve Imprint

www.Rigby.com
1-800-531-5015

"Look at the monkey,"

said Sally.

4

"Look at the bear,"

said Sally.

"Look at the elephant,"
said Sally.

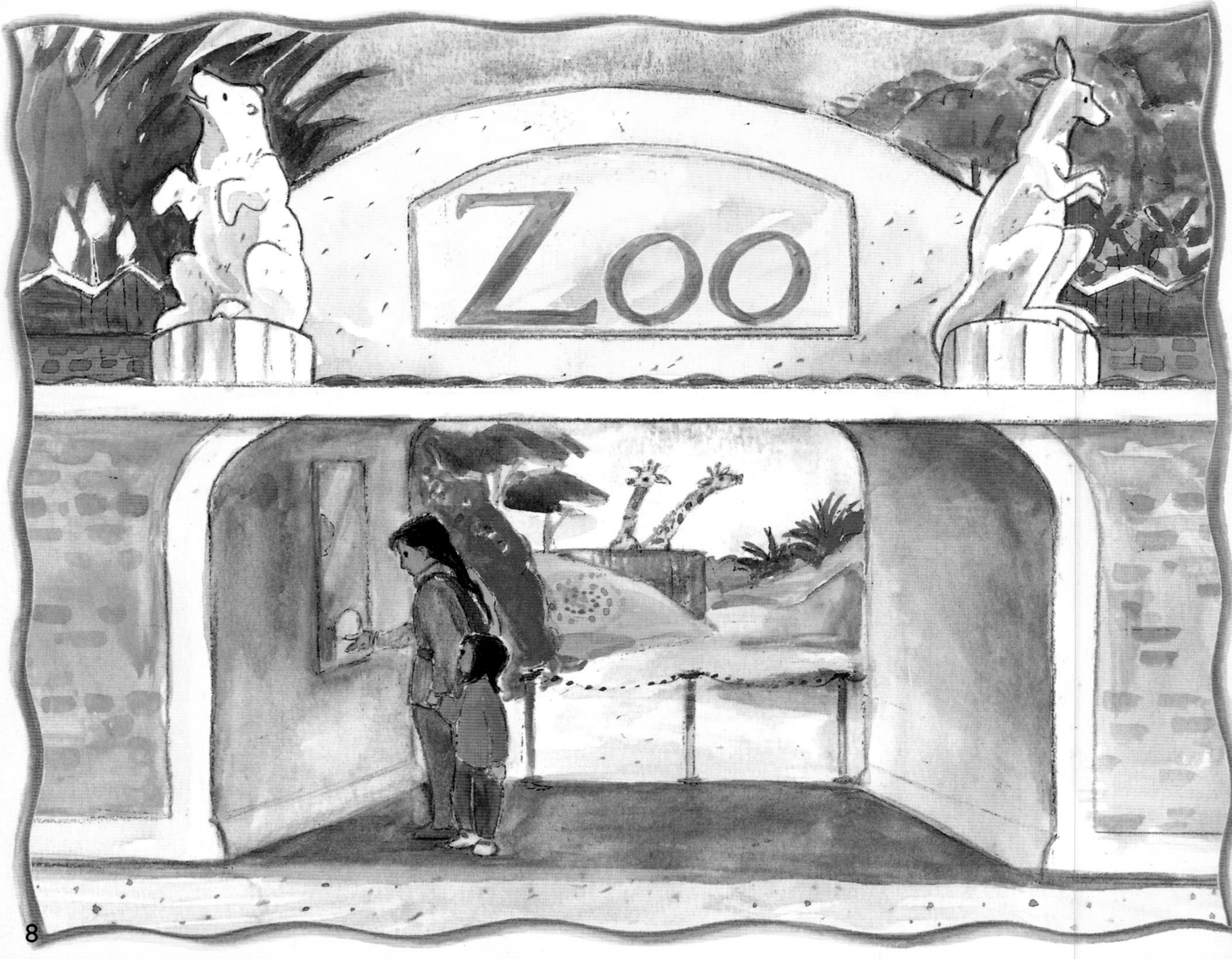
ZOO

Mom and Sally

are at the zoo.

"I can see a monkey,"
said Sally.

"I can see a bear,"

said Mom.

"I can see an elephant!"

said Sally.

"The elephant is **big!**"